FLOWER
Gardening

HANDBOOK FOR BEGINNERS

The Beginner's Guide To Starting A Flower Garden, Getting Ready For Garden Soil, Planting and Maintaining A Flower Garden

Rebecca Moody

Legal & Disclaimer
The information contained in this book is provided for educational purposes only. You understand that this book is not intended to substitute for consultation with a licensed gardener. None of this information should be construed as professional advice. Therefore, by using this information you understand that results will vary, and there are no guarantees or promises in results that come after taking action on any of the educational information presented. The use of this book implies your acceptance of this disclaimer

Neither the author nor the publisher shall be liable or responsible for any loss or adverse effects allegedly arising from any information or suggestion on this book. While every effort has been made to ensure the accuracy of the information presented, neither the authors nor the publisher assumes any responsibility for the error. References are provided for information purposes only and do not constitute an endorsement of any website or other sources.

All images are from freepik.com

Table of contents

1

CHAPTER

Steps to Starting a Flower Garden

Flower gardening as a passionate hobby can be overwhelming, particularly when you first begin. Inexperienced gardeners might not know where to start since there are millions of plants to pick from different combinations.

Start right away, and don't worry if you make mistakes. You can modify your garden over time by removing what did not work and embracing what did. You will find out that garden design plants can make you happy, and learning exactly what it is might be pleasant.

I like choosing which roses, daisies, or larkspur to plant in my walkway as I discover their new colors.

Remember to recycle those plastic pots once every year. Perennials naturally reproduce more than twice as many blooms as they do the previous year. The garden soil gets progressively healthier with each application of manure and compost.

February seems a little less stressful while waiting for the seeds to arrive and planting them close to a window with natural light or under a fluorescent grow lamp. When March finally comes, my seeds grow into small, priceless plants.

Soon enough, spring will arrive, the sun will warm the ground, and it will be time to get your hands filthy. So the whole family can have fun. The entire family can enjoy one of the few pastimes I can think of without requiring you to leave the house or spend money.

Knowing where you want to plant your flowers is the first step in building the ideal flower garden. Pay attention to your natural surroundings to discover the characteristics of your country's soil. Be truthful about the geography, moisture levels, and light.

Knowing your soil

Conducting a soil test is a crucial step in ensuring the success of your flower garden. To collect soil samples, dig a hole one foot deep, collect a few tablespoons, and repeat around your garden until a quart-sized jar is filled. If you want to adjust your soil before planting, you can send it to a testing facility.

Knowing your frost dates

You must be aware of the specific last and first frost dates in your area if you want to ensure that your newly planted garden will endure the changing seasons.

Start your seeds 4 to 6 weeks before the typical last date of the last frost. Weeds will be less abundant as the plants grow more quickly. If you do not have a greenhouse, you can start your seeds indoors in a covered seed tray with grow lights.

Choosing a Color Scheme

Using different shades and shades of the same color can make an effect without being too much. Complementary colors, which are opposites of each other, create a juxtaposition while adhering to a few similar hues that might produce a sensation of harmony. For instance, the color scheme of blue and yellow is cheerful, breezy, and fresh. Warm colors like yellow, orange and red make the most of the light in a sunny area, particularly during the "golden hours," when the sun rises or sets. Hot hues might, however, come off as reasonably flat when used alone. Yellow and blue together create harmony and vitality. The occasional flashes of fiery orange and scarlet offer a little excitement.

Creating Calm Spaces

There is no better way to ease off the stress and tension of each day than to create a cool garden with an ambiance of peace and tranquility where you can relax after a busy day. There is a need to ponder over the structure of your garden as well as the available space where you intend to create the garden.

Whatever works best for you is good - whether to create a curvature using ropes or horticultural sand to balance the boundary or setting some pots at a prominent angle. The height and the growing pattern of your plants is an aspect that should be considered. Color, plant movement and the scent will also help us gain a sense of well-being.

Expert Design

The following basic forms are common in perennials: spires, plumes, daisies, buttons, globes, umbels, and screens. Combine various conditions to see if they spark off one another. While some combinations will conflict, others will be vivid and lively. You can strengthen this notion by planting similar flower shapes together.

Using similar hues or shapes repeatedly creates a sense of tranquility and aesthetic consistency. As you move from one part of the garden to another, the thoughtful repetition of flowers keeps things flowing.

Make layers in your design: Attempt to pull one layer softly into another — and vice versa — to create a more natural effect, rather than just organizing the levels. So it's crucial to maintain sight lines to see the flowers at the back of a border. Plant combinations are more important rather than individual species. The garden is attractive in all seasons because of the variety of plant heights, sizes, colors, scales, and textures. Relaxed plants will add color, motion, and a meadow-like atmosphere.

Taking advantage of natural air patterns to allow the aromas of flowers to drift into your home areas.

Keep stones around the beds if you want your flowers to spill over naturally but do not want them to be in the path of the mower's blades. Also, make wide paths between flowerbeds so that people do not walk through the garden and step on the flowers. Put shrubs in the middle of your flowerbeds to add structure and height all year round and choose smaller cultivars to minimize pruning chores.

Can you envisage your dream garden? You can make it real. Choosing the right garden designs will help you create a cute scheme that you continue to admire many years after. There are lots of fantastic garden ideas that can help reshape and transform your garden into a beautiful one and even increase the market value of your property. With endless design options, these will help you choose the best ones when starting a flower garden, so you can sit back and enjoy the flowers you've grown.

2

CHAPTER

Getting Ready for Garden Soil

G row on a solid base, and you will have healthy, nourishing crops and beautiful flowers every year.

Organic gardens start with good soil. When the garden soil is healthy, less fertilizer and pesticides are required. Soil development improves your plant's health.

Humus, which is a byproduct of decomposing things like leaves, grass clippings, and compost, is abundant in organic soil. It drains efficiently yet retains moisture. Good organic garden soil is fluffy, loose, and full of the air that plant roots require. It contains lots of minerals that are necessary for healthy plant growth. Earthworms, fungi, bacteria, and other living things keep the soil healthy. Another crucial aspect of healthy soil is proper pH.

How can you tell if your soil is healthy, then? In addition, if it isn't, what should you do?

How to Assess Soil Health

The three most important elements are nitrogen, phosphorus, and potassium, out of the roughly 17 elements estimated to be necessary for plant growth. Since plants extract them from the soil in the most significant quantities, they are referred to as "main" or "macroscopic" nutrients. Although complete fertilizers are marketed as having all three nutrients, they are scarcely complete in the strictest sense.

Many plants also require the secondary nutrients calcium, magnesium, and sulfur. The less critical micronutrients are boron, copper, iron, manganese, and zinc. Some plant micronutrients serve unique purposes. For example, cobalt aids legumes in fixing nitrogen even though other plants don't use it. Another crucial aspect is your soil's pH reading, which measures its acid-alkaline balance. Healthy soil is made up of all these components and the right texture.

Soil Testing

Soil Testing is about finding out what minerals are present in it in abundance or deficit. Soil tests at local Cooperative Extension Services are inexpensive. These tests assess the soil's pH, magnesium, phosphorus, calcium, potassium, and occasionally nitrogen levels. They might also provide information on the micronutrient content of the earth, but a gardener who amends her soil with lots of organic matter won't need this. You can go for a less time-consuming test, like the:

Rapid Soil Test Kit.

PH levels significantly influence how your plant can take in nutrients. Plants benefit most from having access to minerals and nutrients in soils with a pH of 6.5 to 6.8. No matter how rich in nutrients your soil is, if it has a low pH (at or below 6.0) or a high pH (above 7.0), the plants will not absorb the nutrients. You can determine the acid-alkaline balance of your soil by purchasing a pH meter, which is typically included in soil tests.

When you should do testing

The soil is most stable in the spring and fall. If your soil lacks minerals or nutrients, now is the perfect time to add any soil amendments or organic fertilizer.

Texture and Soil Type

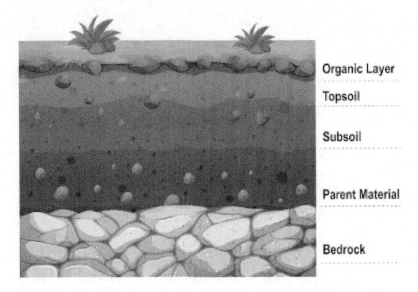

Always check your soil's texture in addition to learning about its pH, macronutrient content, and mineral levels. The amounts of sand, silt, and clay determine the Soil texture. The largest soil particles consist of sand, which has a gritty texture. The silt particles, which are next in size and are powdery while dry, are slippery when wet. Clay makes up the smallest part. They prefer to be stacked like plates or sheets of paper because they are flat. To determine soil texture, you do not need to be an expert. Simply take a small amount and press it between your fingertips. Sand is described as soil that feels grainy. Silty soil has a talcum-powder-like smoothness to it. The ground is heavy clay if it feels rough while dry, slick, and sticky when wet. Most soils will fall in this range.

Since water and nutrients drain quickly through the wide crevices between the sand particles, sandy soils typically have low nutritional levels. Also, these soils often don't have enough organic matter or helpful microorganisms for plants to grow well.

Silty soils are compact and poorly drained. Compared to sandy or clay soils, they are more fertile.

Heavy clay soils tend to be dense, poorly drained, and hard to break when dry. There is typically not much organic matter or microbial life in the ground because there isn't much space between the clay particles. Growing roots is challenging in dense material.

The ideal technique when preparing the soil for planting is to add organic matter in the form of compost and aged manure, use mulch, or cultivate cover crops (green manures). Chemical fertilizers should only be used to restore certain nutrients; they do not affect keeping healthy, friable soil. Everything your plants require is supplied by organic matter.

Air

Plants require air, like people do, both above ground for photosynthesis and in the soil. The soil air contains atmospheric nitrogen, which is changed into a form that plants can use. The life of soil organisms that help plants depends on soil oxygen.

Healthy soil has an ideal amount of space between its particles to hold the air that plants need. silty and heavy clay soils make up closely spaced particles. There is little air in these rich soils. The issue with sandy soils is that the particles are too large and widely spaced. Excess air causes a quick breakdown of organic materials in sandy soil.

Compost balances the air supply when organic matter is added (the perfect soil is about 25 percent air). Also, avoid walking on the beds or using heavy machinery that could compact the soil. Avoid working it when it is damp.

Water

Water is necessary for all living things, including plants and soil organisms, but not in excess or insufficient amounts. Water should make up roughly 25% of healthy soil.

Sandy soils are porous, allowing water to drain and preventing plants from using it quickly. The ground becomes waterlogged when water fills every pore space in thick, silty, or clay soils. Plant roots and soil creatures will perish because of this.

The best soils have pore spaces that are both small and large. A good strategy to strengthen the structure of your soil by encouraging the development of aggregates is to add organic matter (see below). Organic matter also retains water, allowing plants to use it when required.

Soil organisms

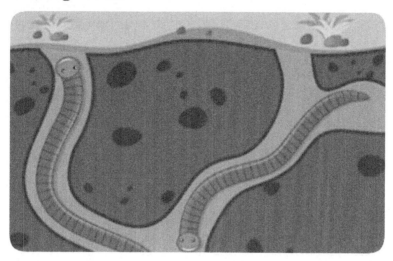

Soil organism comes in various sizes from very minute cells that aid the digestion of decaying organic substances to small ones that live on other organisms on the soil. The presence of these organisms helps to maintain the aeration, fertility, structure, and drainage of the soil. These tiny creatures link soil particles into aggregates that give the earth its loose, fluffy texture and make nutrients available to plants. In soil, you can find earthworms, nematodes, springtails, bacteria, fungi, protozoa, and mites.

Although some of these creatures can be added to the soil, they won't thrive if the conditions aren't right. It is better to provide them with the food (organic matter), air, and water they require to establish an ideal habitat, then let them flourish independently.

Organic Substance

Adding compost to the soil is good. After mixing, the texture of silt and clay soils and their nutrient levels is greatly enhanced. Any soil will improve with yearly treatments on top. You can make your organic compost at home or buy it by the bag or in the yard.

Compost and other organic compounds serve as aggregates that keep soil particles together and aid in moisture retention. Also, they take in and store nutrients that plants can then use, and compost feeds microbes that help plants.

Creating your compost can be as simple as placing green trash, like grass clippings, on top of brown waste, such as straw and leaves. Turn the pile frequently and keep it moist.

We have composters and bins you can buy to keep your vegetable scraps and make turning easier if you are worried about mice and other animals getting into your bank.

Mulch

Straw, hay, grass clippings, and shredded bark are organic materials that cover the soil and protect it from harsh heat and cold. Mulching inhibits the growth of weeds and lessens water loss due to evaporation. They decompose gradually, adding organic matter to the soil.

Pebbles, gravel, black plastic, and landscape fabrics work like organic mulches to slow evaporation and control weed growth. They do not need to be changed often and aren't attracted to pests like organic mulches. However, inorganic mulches do not help the soil by decomposing and introducing organic matter that enhances soil structure and nutrient content. Use a clean, seed-free, high-quality garden mulch if you want to strengthen the structure of your soil.

Fertilizer

Fertilizers, whether dry or liquid, can supply nutrients to the soil that might not otherwise reach it. Although they work a little bit slower than their synthetic counterparts, organic garden fertilizers deliver their nutrients over a more extended period. In addition, synthetic fertilizers hurt the environment and could eventually lower the quality of the soil by killing off microbes that are good for it.

The soil is restored by adding dry organic fertilizers and watering. Compared to liquid fertilizers, they act slowly but have a lasting effect. Different combinations of nitrogen, phosphorous, and potassium are found in fertilizers. The label includes the ratio (for example, 5-10-5). They contain bat guano, rock phosphate, molasses, and other components in various fertilizers. Most of them are a variation of the nitrogen, phosphorus, and potassium themes with extra nutrients from seed meals, ash, lime, greensand, or other mineral specks of dust and additional organic components, frequent kelp, leaf mold, or dried manure.

Liquid nutrients are sprayed on the soil or the plant's foliage. Anglers frequently use fish emulsion and seaweed mixtures as organic liquid fertilizers. Another way to make liquid fertilizer that uses the compost that is amassing in your yard is compost tea. Try soaking the underside of the leaves if you are using a foliar spray. The stomata, the tiny pores that allow gases to enter the plant, are found here. They will swiftly absorb the fertilizer as it spread to let in carbon dioxide and release moisture. Read the labels of the liquid fertilizer you select because certain products should only be used on soil and may burn crops.

Cover Crops

Cover crops give essential organic matter to the soil while assisting in wind and erosion protection. They are typically planted in the fall. They create a dense root system that may improve the texture of the soil. In addition to controlling weeds, cover crops also help fix nitrogen and ward off pests and diseases.

The crops become green manure when incorporated into the soil. Alfalfa and rye are typical cover crops.

In the case of winter cover crops, cover crops are sown either towards the conclusion of the growing season or throughout a portion of it (summer cover crops). In summer green crop legumes like cowpeas, soybeans, annual sweet clover, or velvet beans are grown to supply nitrogen and organic matter. Non-legumes are planted to produce biomass, smother weeds, and enhance soil tilt. Examples include millet, buckwheat, forage sorghum, and sorghum-sudangrass.

Winter cover crops are sown in the late summer or early fall to cover the soil during the off-season. For the added benefit of nitrogen fixation, use a legume crop. Growers in northern states should use cover crops with sufficient cold tolerance to withstand harsh winters, such as hairy vetch and rye. The southern United States can support a lot more winter cover crops. Field peas, vetches, clovers, and medics are examples of cool-season legumes. They are occasionally sown in a mixture of winter cereal grains like rye, wheat, or oats.

Add compost and any other soil amendments (like lime) you think your soil needs after you've finished harvesting your summer crops. Spread the cover crop seeds, then softly rake. Plant cover crop seeds between the rows of vegetables if you wish to continue growing them into the fall, at least one month before you anticipate harvesting them.

Allowing your cover crops to go to seed could make them invasive. Till the harvest into the soil 2-3 weeks before planting when spring arrives. Using a rototiller to integrate cover crops into the ground is simple.

PH

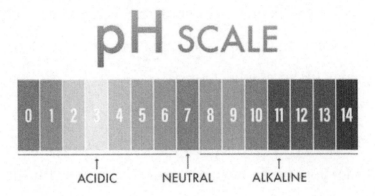

The acidity or alkalinity of soil is determined by a pH test. A reading of 7.0 using the pH meter is neutral. Anything below 7.0 is acidic and anything above 7.0 is alkaline.

Any soil with a pH level between 3.0-5.0 is very acidic and nutrients like copper, calcium, magnesium, and potassium can be eroded quickly and easily. Some phosphate cannot be effective in soils having an acidity of 5.1 and above and will lack trace elements. Also, bacteria cannot effectively decompose organic matter at a pH that is lower than 4.7. This will affect the supply of nutrients to the plant. To remedy this, add lime to increase the PH to above 5.0.

When you have a reading between 7.1 to 8.0, the soil is alkaline. This reduces the amount of phosphorus, manganese, and iron available in the soil. One good advantage of this pH range is that it reduces clubroot diseases of brassicas. Adding sulphur or iron sulphate can be added to normalize the pH value.

The pH of your soil cannot be easily altered. It should take one or two seasons to moderate the pH and then work each year to keep it that way. Adding a lot of organic matter each year will help the soil become more balanced, regardless of how acidic or alkaline it is.

Limestone powder can be put on acidic soil in the fall as a buffer. (Since it takes several months to work, autumn is the best time to do this.) While most plants do not thrive in acidic soil, some do, such as azaleas and blueberries.

To raise the pH of sandy soil by about a point, add 3-4 pounds of ground limestone per 100 square feet. Add limestone at a rate of 7-8 pounds per 100 feet for loamy soil and 8–10 pounds per 100 feet for heavy clay soil. Apply at least two to three months before planting to give limestone time to work.

Wood ash increases soil pH, but you must cautiously use it. Too much wood ash could raise pH levels and deplete your soil's nutrients. In the fall, only lightly sprinkle your earth with fertilizer; turn the ground over entirely in the spring. When seeds meet ash, they might not sprout. If you use wood ash every year, pay close attention to the pH of your soil and stop using it when taking the correct reading.

On the other hand, it is necessary to increase the acidity of alkaline soil. Accomplish this with Sulfur, sawdust, conifer needles, sawdust, or oak leaves. Apply 1 pound of ground sulfur per 100 feet to sandy soil, 1.5–2 pounds per 100 feet to loamy soil, and 2 pounds per 100 feet to heavy clay soils, you can reduce the pH by about one point.

Grass Texture

Add 3-4 inches of organic matter (such as compost) to make sandy soil less sandy. Use mulch around plants made of wood chips, leaves, hay, straw, or bark, and add at least 2 inches of organic material each year. Avoid walking on or tilling the ground until required to avoid compacting it. Silty soil can be used effectively in raised beds without requiring intensive growing.

2-3 inches of organic matter incorporated into heavy clay soil will improve it. Then every year, raise the top by another inch or more. Raised beds will facilitate better drainage and prevent soil compaction from occurring from foot traffic. Don't wait until it's essential.

It reduces the pH of alkaline soils! 90% of Elemental Sulfur is sulfur, while 10% of it is bentonite, which serves as a binder. It is also helpful as a soil improvement around acid-loving plants like blueberries, azaleas, and rhododendrons.

Typically, bone meal is advised to increase soil phosphorous levels, whereas blood meal is reported to increase soil nitrogen levels. Butchering facilities produced both of these. Thankfully, there are several options.

Try alfalfa meal or alfalfa pellets instead of blood meal or fish emulsion (sold for rabbit food). Alternatively, use alfalfa as a cover crop to provide plants with nitrogen. Alfalfa is a good compost accelerator and contributes little phosphorus and potassium.

Cottonseed meal, available at your neighborhood feed shop and adds nitrogen to the soil, is similar to alfalfa pellets. However, it is somewhat acidic, so unless you want to lower the pH of the soil, use it in conjunction with lime.

To raise phosphorous levels, substitute soft-rock phosphate for bone meal.

A side note: Adding alfalfa or cottonseed meal to the soil isn't truly "organic" unless you can find it in an organic form. Cotton and alfalfa seeds not produced organically may have pesticide and herbicide residues.

3

CHAPTER

Planting for beginners

Direct planting is the process of putting roots into the ground of an outdoor garden. No specialized gear is required, and there aren't any little pots or flats to play around with. You don't need to be concerned about hardening off your plants or transplanting them or the associated risk of transplant shock.

This does not imply that direct planting is risk-free or the best technique for all plants. Tomatoes, peppers, and eggplants are plants that do not grow well when directly sown in areas with chilly climates. Additionally, it is advisable to start plants indoors that require highly specialized germination conditions. But you can plant a surprising number of fruits, vegetables, annuals, and perennials in your yard.

Step 1: Select a Location

Where would you like your flower garden to be? Check the areas of your garden that receive the greatest sun. Choose a location that will receive at least six hours of direct sunshine each day because most flowers prefer a sunny location. If possible, you should keep the wind off this area that receives direct sunlight.

Step 2: Begin Tilling

Once you have chosen a location, clear it of any grass, rocks, or other obstructions that may be there. Start chopping up the grass with a shovel. Use a tiller to make the soil more pliable once the grass is removed. Get some high-quality garden soil and combine it with the local dirt. Add some organic compost to the soil to improve it and retain moisture.

Step 3. Planting

We advise starting with perennials for new gardeners because these plants will yield yearly. Be sure to adhere to the instructions on the packets no matter what kind of flowers you select! Plant the flower's root ball in the hole after digging it twice as deep as the container it arrived in. Refill the hole with soil, then compact it.

Study the instructions the plant comes with if you opt to start from seed. Different flowers require various soil types, attention, and exposure to sunlight.

Step 4: Watering

You need to master the art of watering right after planting. Poor watering can hurt your plants. Too much water can attract fungus while inadequate watering can make the root shallow. You invite insects when you water in the evening. As simple as watering sounds, it is a no-brainer. Follow the instructions on the packet in doing this. Observe the guidelines when taking care of your plants. Others may not, depending on the plant.

Step 5: Mulching

Mulching is an excellent idea for most plants. In addition to preventing most weeds from growing, this keeps the soil well-moist, so you will not need to water as frequently. It is crucial to know how to grow flowers if you want to create a beautiful garden.

Always plant after the final frost date. Most plants need to be planted once the soil has warmed up or after the last frost date, depending on the flower you are planting. Some flowers need to be planted before the last frost date.

What design do you want? For example, raised garden beds are simple to maintain and can serve as a pet barrier. Build your garden bed by purchasing the necessary supplies at your neighborhood garden center.

Choose a design that you will love because it can stay for a very long time. Consider window boxes or hanging baskets if you live in a tiny space. Ensure your flowerbed is always in a sunny location. When it is time to plant, be sure to read the instructions carefully and have all of your flower bulbs ready. We believe these gardening tips will make it simple for you to plant your first flower garden.

Most plants thrive in "loamy" soil, which has a balanced ratio of sand, clay, and silt. It is frequently advised to supplement your soil with organic material such as compost, whether it is particularly dense (clay) or highly permeable (sand). Suppose the pH of your soil is too acidic or alkaline to support the growth of the plants you want. The best method to understand your soil and what amendments might be required is to have it analyzed by your university's Extension Service or a commercial testing facility.

What you'll need

- Tools and Resources
- Vegetable fork
- Rake
- Trowel
- mist-setting hose sprayer.
- Materials
- Planting seeds
- Markers for plants and string

Prepare the soil.

Start with flat, weed-free ground that is loose. Spend some time clearing the area of weeds, rocks, and sticks. Also, break up any large clumps of earth. With a garden fork, loosen the soil, apply soil amendments, and rake the area to create a level, even surface.

Using a recent soil test, you can find out the makeup of your garden soil. The test will inform you of the amendments required to create the ideal soil conditions for the plants you want to cultivate. By completely incorporating some organic matter, such as compost that has been properly decomposed, peat moss, or manure, virtually any soil will be enhanced. However, you don't want the soil to be too rich because some seeds do not thrive in excessively fertile soil.

Get the seeds ready (if needed)

Some seeds may benefit from previous preparation. For instance, before planting, some plant species' seeds need to be somewhat softened by soaking them in water. Others might require "scarification" by being run over fine sandpaper. Scarifying the hard shells of some seeds makes it easier for them to take in water, germinate, and grow sprouts.

The following seeds should be scarified: lupine, nasturtium, sweet pea, and morning glory. Some plants, such as perennials like milkweed, require a period of cold and moisture to germinate. This process is known as stratification. You can copy nature by putting these seeds in a container with a moist seed starting mix and putting them in the refrigerator, as it frequently happens naturally when seeds drop from a parent plant and transit through the cold, rainy winter to weaken the seed coat.

Tip

Over time, commercial seeds will progressively lose their ability to germinate. A three-year-old packet of seeds might only have a germination rate of 50% or less, whereas a brand-new pack of sources might have a germination rate of 90%. Saving a few seeds is fine, but remember that you might need to plant the seeds more densely to get enough germination and sprouting.

Keep the soil moist.

Maintaining a consistent moisture level in the soil after seeding is the most crucial step. Letting the soil dry out is the single most significant barrier to germination. However, you do need to rinse a little bit carefully. If you surface-sowed your seeds, a vigorous hose blow will either entirely wash them out of the bed or muck with the spacing. Use the "shower" setting on a hose wand or the "rose" fitting on a watering can to provide your seeds with a gentle stream of water.

Mark the Spots

Mark the spot where you sowed the seeds. For this, small craft sticks marked with permanent ink work great. This is significant whether you are sowing vegetables in your edible garden or have recently planted new annual or perennial seeds in an established ornamental border. As the planting season advances, marking seed placements allows you to keep track of your garden's layout and germination process. Without clear markers, it's too easy to pick "weeds" that are your newly sprouted seedlings by mistake or pack your seeds with different plants.

Know the appearance of your seedlings. It might be challenging to distinguish a weed from a tomato seedling when they have just started. The cotyledons, often known as "seed leaves," are the earliest leaves that develop. To identify your plants correctly, wait until a set of genuine leaves emerges. You can check out websites to view images of certain seedlings, and some seed packets include pictures or illustrations. Knowing the characteristics of your seedlings helps to prevent accidental weed removal.

Your sprouted seedlings might be thinned to maintain the ideal spacing for developing to maturity. This is especially true for seeds that are so small they can only be sprayed over the prepared soil, like celery or carrots. Soon after the seeds sprout, thinning can start since if they are allowed to grow too close, they will not be able to develop into concrete plants.

Find out the ideal distance between plants, and make sure to thin the plants out carefully to prevent upsetting the delicate new roots of nearby plants. Some gardeners prefer to pinch or snip the seedlings off at the ground instead of pulling them out, so they don't disturb the soil.

As the plants enlarge and crowd one another, you might need to think again. The seedlings removed during thinning are a great compliment to salads and other dishes with many veggies.

Tip

Many plants, particularly flowering annuals, easily self-seed by dispersing their mature flower heads' seeds. For instance, you might discover that the previous year's snapdragons, zinnias, foxgloves, or marigolds did all of your direct sowing for you. This is especially true if your usual practice was not to deadhead the flowers but let them go to seed. You will need to thin out self-seeded plants to prevent your garden from becoming overrun with volunteers because they frequently spring up in thick clusters of seedlings. If plants grow where you don't want them, even the most beautiful ones quickly start to look like weeds.

Maintain the seedlings.

Young seedlings require special care for the first few weeks due to their fragility, especially when it comes to maintaining wet soil. In general, it's a good idea to spray plants with water daily, although hot weather may call for twice-daily watering.

Feeding is typically postponed until the plant is large enough to start setting flower buds. Some seed packets for plants tell you to feed them diluted fertilizer for the first month or so after you plant them until they are strong enough to handle full-strength fertilizer.

Also, make sure to weed the area around your young seedlings thoroughly. Weeds will compete with plants for nutrition, sunlight, and water. Therefore, routine weeding is a necessity.

Troubleshooting

If your garden is struggling and not growing as expected, use these gardening troubleshooting tips to help identify the issue and apply the appropriate solution to it.

Only 25% of my seeds sprouted. What happened?

Several things impact seed germination. Check the seed packaging to ensure that all of the conditions for temperature and light were met. The seeds might have rotted if the soil was too cold and moist. Examine one of the seeds you dug up. The seed has rotted if it is bloated and squishy, so you must start over. The sources might not have germinated or dried out before their roots could take hold if the soil were too dry. The seeds might not be still alive if they were old. Retry and make sure to supply constant moisture.

My Sprouts are Skinny. What should I do?

Darkness causes plants to become tall and skinny. Use grow lamps to ensure they get 15 hours of bright sunshine daily. Additionally, warm weather might promote awkward development. Reduce the temperature in the room and the amount of fertilizer you use.

My tomato plants' leaves are beginning to turn purple along the veins and underside. What is going on?

When a plant has purple leaves, it is not getting enough phosphorus and potassium. Potassium helps in photosynthesis (a process where plants get energy from sunlight). The deficiency of phosphorus in the soil can lead to the leaves turning purple or dark green. You can remedy the deficiencies by adding fertilizer that is high in potassium and phosphorus.

My seedlings were flourishing until the root collapsed. What took place?

Young seedlings that have their stems wither and fall over have likely succumbed to "damping off," a fungus that lives in the soil. You can avoid this condition by ensuring your seeds have enough light, well-prepared, and drained soil. You must be wary of overwatering, excessive shade, and the use of excess fertilizer. If you detect it, apply a fungicide solution immediately.

On the top of the soil's surface, mold is developing. Although it doesn't seem to be harming my plants, should I be worried?

The presence of mold indicates that the growing medium is very moist. As long as you take action, it won't hurt your plants. Withhold water for a few days while attempting to use a tiny fan to improve airflow around the containers. Additionally, you can try moving the seedlings into new soil or attempting to scrape some of the molds off. Even though direct sowing is a risky practice influenced by the weather and local fauna, the substantial cost savings make the rare failure a reasonable price to pay. The cost of starting a garden from direct-sown seeds is considerably less than creating a garden from potted nursery plants.

When Should I Directly Sow in My Garden?

Your region's climate and the plant you are growing will determine when to plant your seeds. People can plant many vegetable seeds as soon as the spring frost has completely melted and the soil is workable, but some sources might need warmer soil to guarantee germination and sprouting. Depending on the environment and the seed, certain seeds can be sown in the fall. To find out the ideal planting period for the seeds you wish to grow, research the plant species and read the specifications mentioned on the seed packaging.

Each plant species has unique preferences for soil type, planting season, amount of sunlight and water, and other aspects of maintenance. To discover these preferences, research the species you intend to grow. It's possible that only a portion of your garden is suited or that your soil type calls for additional soil additions.

4

Garden Maintenance

After growing your garden, the next phase that will determine its success is its maintenance. Owning a garden is as important as ensuring its consistent maintenance. Maintenance of your garden should be regular and not occasional exercise. For your garden to florish, frequent care is paramount. Pay close attention while taking a routine walk around your garden just to ensure everything is fine. It will be easy to discover any issue with your plants if you frequent your garden, this will enable you to take the necessary action to remedy it.

Hygiene

Keep your garden clean. Leaving decayed vegetation around your garden is an invitation for many pests and diseases. Do not hesitate to take away plant debris from time to time and dispose of them properly. Having pets, and kids or hosting social gatherings might cause your garden space to get dirty, unkempt, or otherwise harmed. Hidden furniture or shed spaces may have mold, rot, or other problems. Do well to take care of the area where your garden is located.

Weed control

Weeds can constitute a nuisance and serve as a breeding ground for pests and insects if you allow them in your garden. They are garden killers. They can share soil nutrients with your plants and can stunt their growth. Constant weeding of your garden will keep diseases at bay especially when you weed at the start of every growing season.

Thoroughly inspect plants Before buying.

The easiest way to lessen the effect of disease on your garden is to prevent its entrance in the first place. Don't be in a hurry to buy plants, be patient to inspect them, looking out for signs like holes in the leave, blisters, black or brown spots, or distorted leaves as a result of pest or disease infection. One of the hardest things to understand is what a healthy plant should look like, so it might be difficult to tell whether the plant you want is sick.

It's a great idea to compile a few catalogs that feature pictures of healthy specimens. You should not bring home a plant with insects, decaying stems, or dead spots. Once these problems start, they can spread quickly to your healthy plants and can be hard to get rid of.

Always check the roots of plants in addition to the crowns for quality. Place your hand on the ground while holding the plant stem in your fingers. Turn the pot upside down and gently shake the plant loose. You might need to tap the pot's edge on a hard surface to get the roots out. Check to see if the tips of the plant appear healthy, a plant with a decaying root system will eventually die.

Use only fully composted waste.

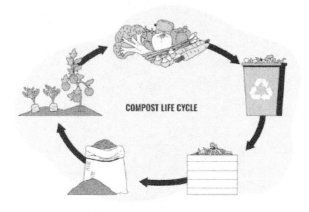

COMPOST LIFE CYCLE

Compost pile materials don't decompose at the same rate. Some might have decayed sufficiently to be utilized in the garden, but not others. Many pathogens are eliminated by the prolonged high temperatures created by thorough composting. Diseases might be reintroduced into your garden through plant debris from diseased plants that have not undergone this treatment. When mulching sensitive plants, stay away from using yard waste, and if you are not sure how healthy your compost pile is, do not add possibly contagious materials.

Watch out for insects.

Insect damage to plants affects more than just the roots. It causes openings that viruses and bacteria typically need to penetrate a plant. In reality, certain insects carry viruses that spread from one plant to the next. The necrotic spot virus, a substantial problem for commercial growers over the past ten years, is distributed this way. One of the common vectors is aphids. Leafhoppers disseminate Aster yellows, which have an extensive range of host plants as their victims. Insect infestations can also stress a plant and weaken its defenses against disease.

Clean up in the fall.

It is better to clean up the garden in the fall, even if you live in a region with warm temperatures. This is a fantastic way to stay healthy and also control diseases already present in your garden.

Diseases can hibernate on dead leaves and other debris, then attack new leaves when they emerge in the spring. You can significantly reduce iris leaf spots, daylily leaf streaks, and black spots on roses if the fallen leaves are removed each fall. Remove any stems and foliage left over during winter before the start of the new growth in the spring.

Apply a good fertilizer

Be cautious while applying fertilizing plants since too much fertilizer will burn roots, reducing their ability to absorb water. As a result, the plants are more susceptible to heat, cold, and drought stress. While nutrient-starved plants are smaller and more prone to leaf spots, more vigorous plants can resist disease. A plant can also become stressed out by receiving a large amount of a particular nutrient.

A soil test to give you exact information on the nutrient levels in your soil is important. Without it, feeding your plants would likely require guesswork, which could give them too much of one nutrient or not enough.

Employ disease-resistant species.
Disease-resistant plants are susceptible to diseases but fend them off rather than succumb to them. For example, some tomato varieties are listed as "VFN resistant," which means they are resistant to Fusarium, Verticillium, and Nematodes.

If you start looking for these flower codes, you could be disappointed because disease resistance is rarely noted on plant tags. This is not to say that all flower cultivars are susceptible to disease. Many rose growers offer bushes that can fend off diseases like powdery mildew and black spot. Many plant species have their best or most resilient varieties, which nursery staff and other gardeners may help you identify.

Trim Broken Branches.

Trimming trees and shrubs in the late winter is preferable to doing it in the spring. Late winter pruning prevents the infection from affecting new growth. Removing a broken part now is still advisable rather than waiting until spring, even though late-winter storms may cause more significant harm. Always use sharp tools and clean, rapid cuts to ensure that only healthy, living tissue is left.

Choose your Plant wisely.

The secret to gardening success is selecting appropriate plants for your region and climate. If planted in full sun, a plant that prefers shade, such as an azalea, may grow poorly and be more vulnerable to pests and disease. I once planted a crape myrtle that had some of its leaves shaded. The plant's powdery mildew was restricted to this particular location.

Plants have defenses that activate when attacked by an insect or disease, much like a person's immune system does. When plants are stressed, they are less able to fight off diseases or recover from them. As a result, they are more vulnerable to contracting these diseases.

Water Properly.

Watering your garden is a good idea, but since many diseases also need water to survive, how you go about it is very important. Most soil and air pathogens require water to move, develop, and reproduce. Use watering methods that leave the least moisture on a plant's leaves to avoid giving these diseases a perfect home. Drip irrigation and soaker hoses are used to accomplish this. If you are watering by hand, keep the leaves out of the way while you water the roots.

Because wet leaves exacerbate the most common leaf problems, overhead sprinkling is the least optimal option; nevertheless, if you choose to use this strategy, do it when the leaves are going to dry out quickly, while the roots still have time to absorb the water before it evaporates.

Kindly note that more water isn't always better when watering your plants. Some fungi that cause roots to rot can grow in wet soil or pots and suffocate roots, making them easy prey for the fungi.

Make sure your plants are evenly spaced.
Removing crowded, broken, or old stalks from plants prone to powdery mildew is advisable. When plants are too close, they make it easier for diseases like powdery mildew to grow.

Consider the spacing between transplants, and keep an eye on how quickly existing plants are growing. Downy mildew, rust, and powdery mildew can flourish on crowded plants because they create humidity. By increasing airflow around your plants, you can lower this high relative humidity while simultaneously hastening the drying of the leaves.

When plants grow too closely together, they compete with one another for nutrients, water, and light, stunting their growth. It is more likely that an infected leaf will come into contact with a healthy one.

Remove crowded, broken, or old stalks from plants like Phlox paniculata susceptible to powdery mildew to lower the chance of sickness. You can divide or rearrange your plants if they need it.

5 | Cutting Beautiful Blooms

You can easily make a bed, which can produce enough flowers to fill vases from spring to autumn if you know the best cut garden flowers to plant at home. Mix up the colors, shapes, and sizes for a dazzling look in a flower garden; alternatively, use a small color palette for a cozier effect.

Making a small hole in the earth, putting bulbs pointed side up, covering them with soil, and waiting for them to grow are all necessary. Starting a cutting garden is with annuals (plants that bloom and die within a year), as they simply need a light sprinkle of seed in a seed tray or on the ground. Although cultivating perennials may require a bit more effort and patience, they are worth the commitment.

From saucer-sized dahlias in bright pinks, purples, and oranges to lacy spires of color like delphiniums, lupins, and gladioli, the best-cut garden flowers come in a variety of sizes and forms. There are bright open-faced cosmos as well as button-shaped flowers like astrantia. Selecting primarily "cut and come again" flowers are the secret to a productive cutting garden. With these blooms, it's a win-win situation since the more you select, the more flowers they'll grow. You will enjoy fresh flowers in your home.

Peas

Sweet peas are the epitome of an English-cut flower, with their ruffled petals, vibrant colors, and tendrils of foliage. These hardy annual climber plants require a support structure, ideally a cane wigwam. Garden centers sell young plants in April, but you may also learn how to start sweet peas from seed.

Plant them in deep root containers, which give them the depth they require in the fall or spring. For a more robust, bushier plant, pinch the growing tips when they reach a height of about 4 inches (10 cm).

When it's time to plant sweet peas (about mid-April), dig in a lot of compost first since they are hungry. Fix them to the supports as they grow and keep the soil moist.

Choose the blossoms as they appear in the early to late summer; the more you pick, the more they produce. The sweet pea variety "Mollie Rhilstone" is a favorite of Northamptonshire-based florist Tracey Mathieson, who also has her cutting garden. It has softly colored petals, a strong scent, and straight, long stems that are perfect for vases.

Sunflowers

Sunflowers are the loveliest garden flowers to cut. If you're searching for a surefire flower to start a cutting patch, sunflowers are a great choice because they add a dash of sunshine to a plain jug on a kitchen table.

Simply plant them where you want them to grow and then watch them grow naturally. Choose a plant with multiple heads that will produce lots of flowers. You should give "Harlequin," "Vanilla Ice," and a tawny variety called "Red Sun" a try. When the young plants are developing, be on the lookout for slugs.

It would be best if you cut sunflowers before the blooms are fully opened, and you should permanently remove the lowest leaves from the stems before placing them in water.

Dahlias

Understanding how to grow dahlias is good if you want a late summer burst of color. They blossom up to the first frosts and come in a spectrum of jewel tones. Dahlia tubers may appear aged, but do not let that deter you; they are easy to grow.

There are two approaches. If you have the space, one tuber should be planted in each pot, under glass, in late winter or early spring, and when the weather warms up, you may put them outside. If your climate is similar to that of the UK, plant the tubers directly in the ground once the risk of frost has passed. This usually happens in early May.

Protect them using a covering of mulch and left in the ground during the winter in milder climates. Once the first frosts have turned the foliage black in colder climates, some gardeners pluck the tubers. You can dry them indoors and store them in a small tray until planting.

"Chat Noir" Dahlia

For vases, I prefer smaller single flowers, blooms that resemble water lilies, and cactus varieties like this long-stemmed, deep-red cultivar with pointed, narrow petals. Dahlias are a wise investment because they keep growing yearly, although they may need to be lifted and stored in a frost-free environment if deep frosts are frequent.

Dahlias will fail in a vase if the last inch of the stem is not immediately plunged into hot water for 20 seconds after cutting.

Cosmos

There are so many kinds of cosmos to pick from, and seed producers are constantly producing new varieties. Choose from the plain white variety with solitary flowers on long branches or the vibrant, frilly Pink Popsocks.

Annual cosmos are best sown in seed modules in April undercover. They start growing in a week or less. Keep one healthy seedling per module; when it starts getting skinny, pinch out the growth tips. In a sunny location, plant in the middle to end of May. From June until October, the cosmos will bloom. If you keep cutting the blossoms, they will continue to bloom for you.

Apricot Lemonade: Cosmos bipinnatus

Cosmos bipinnatus 'Apricot Lemonade' are delicate apricots that turn pink in the center. They contrast beautifully with elaborate leaves from midsummer to midfall, and the plants are compact for container planting and have lengthy stems. These showy Mexicans do well when planted 12 inches (30 cm) apart and raised under glass. Try bundling them with a ladies' mantle and cherry-colored penstemon.

Lily

Lilies are an excellent option for cut garden flowers since they have robust, tall stems and numerous blossoms. They are an easy choice since they grow from bulbs. Although there are many distinct lily species, Asiatic hybrids are the easiest to grow.

Anytime between October and March, plant the bulbs in the sun or partial shade. Place the bulbs pointed side up in a hole 8 inches (20 cm) deep. Keep them in groups of 3 or 5 to create a more natural impression. To ensure proper drainage, strew some grit into the hole.

Once established, lilies will reappear year after year, giving the cutting garden an air of exoticism. Keep a third of the stem attached when cutting a lily since this will nourish the bulb for the following year.

Astrantia

These delicate, understated blossoms are a lovely complement to a bouquet of cut flowers. They can reach a height of 35 inches and have tidy, button-shaped flowers on robust stalks (90cm).

Astrantia is a perennial plant that is best purchased from a garden center as a young plant rather than raised from seed. Plant them in the spring in moist, healthy soil shaded by dappled light. One of the Astrantia varieties that blooms the longest and can withstand drier circumstances is "Buckland," which has a pale pink blossom.

Gladioli

Gladiolus are towering, showy flowers commonly referred to as "sword lilies," which will make a big impression in a cutting garden. You can plant by creating a trench, filling it with well-rotted manure, and then setting the corms inside, about 4 inches (10 cm) apart and 4-6 inches (10-15 cm) deep.

Keep your gladioli well-watered because they do require moisture in addition to rich soil. The plants can be left in the ground over the winter in milder climates since a heavy layer of mulch will provide them with the necessary protection. They will need lifting and drying over the winter in the colder regions of the UK and other similar climates.

Sweet William

Sweet williams are hardy flowers, despite their attractive appeal for cottage garden designs. They grow very slowly (up to 15 inches/40 cm). They are best placed in front of your garden borders. You will find thick clusters of flowers on branched stems.

After the dirt has been finely raked, you can plant the seeds directly into the earth. Go for a sunny location. Beginning in May, draw some memorable lines and sow the seed slowly and as evenly as possible. Since sweet williams are biennial plants, it takes two years for them to blossom, but the wait is well worth it.

Don't be tempted to pick every single one, even if they make lovely cut flowers. They will self-pollinate the following year if you leave a few bloom heads on the plants. Consider "Nigricans" for a deep, velvety purple or "Auricula Eyed Mix" for mauve petals with a light center.

Tulips

Tulips do not produce flowers that can be taken and grown again, but they add a pleasant burst of color before the rest of the garden gets going.

They love the sunlight shade location because they are grown from bulbs. Remember that you should plant tulip bulbs in bunches of at least six or seven for maximum impact.

Allow your tulips to turn brown and die back for about six weeks when they have stopped blooming because this is when the bulbs store food, and it increases the likelihood that the tulips will return with more blossoms the following year.

Put a dime in the water if your cut tulips flop in the vase; they will soon stand tall again. Since they are thirsty, flowers replenish them every day.

Ammi Majus

Their beautiful white blossoms, sometimes referred to as "posh cow parsley," form dreamy clouds and appear nearly hovering over a vase.

Good, well-drained soil guarantees a show of fern-like foliage and umbels of white flowers. Sow seeds directly into the ground or into modules 12 inches (30 cm) apart in the spring. Plant cornflowers in a container at 6-inch (15 cm) intervals for a bouquet-like appearance. Pets may be poisoned by it and irritate their skin.

Keep watering during drought since they enjoy moist soil, moderate shade, and sunlight. Ammi is a tall plant that can reach a height of 3 ft. (1 m), making it an excellent choice for the flowerbed's rear.

Zinnias

Brilliant half-hardy zinnias, which have their roots in Mexico, take pleasure in growing in warm, protected environments.

Make direct sowings into warm, healthy soil well-drained by late spring, and they will blossom from midsummer through fall.

The Zinnia flower has long vase life and comes with large blooms usually in purple. It can be as tall as

75cm with straight stems that will rarely bend even when cut. During hot seasons, they bloom and become attracted to butterflies and bees.

Snapdragons

Tiny snapdragon seeds need to be planted in late winter or early spring. They should be spread out thinly, lightly covered, and allowed to germinate at 60–65 °F (15–18 °C).

To prevent any disease from spreading, keep seedlings cool and well-lit. Before potting, move them into a seed tray in a grid pattern. By ordering young plants, the fiddle is avoided for spires of softly scented bicolored cherry and white blooms all summer; space your plants 12 inches (30 cm) apart.

Gypsophila paniculata Bristol Fairy

Herbaceous perennial baby's breath, which has its origins in Central and Eastern Europe, is a traditional favorite for cut flowers. Gypsophila is a perennial double-white flower that is prevalent in summer. It gives that nice ambiance with an airy bloom with appealing combinations that gives that excellent contrast.

Growing it is easy. Loamy, sandy, and chalky soil is best for planting Gysophila within a PH balance that is neutral or alkaline. Gysophila needs to be exposed to full sunlight with the soil well enriched with compost. Water adequately and evenly. For moisture level to be retained, add a layer of mulch to the soil. Do not forget to space the plants to allow for space to spread as they grow. A spacing of 60cm is ideal.

Phlox Paniculata

Although herbaceous perennials have shorter flowering times than annuals, they are nonetheless valuable additions to the foundation of a cutting garden.

Phlox flowers perform best when exposed to sunlight, they can also do well with some shades, especially in some very hot climates. To grow well, it requires fertile soil that is well stocked with compost or any good organic substance on the ground with an alkaline ph scale. You can plant it in the ground during spring after the adverse effects of frost are subsided. Give proper spacing like 20 inches to allow circulation of air. Watering properly shouldn't be taken lightly.

What Advantages Do Cutting Gardens Offer?

The benefits of starting a cutting garden goes beyond maintaining a consistent supply of flowers. Being surrounded by flowers daily is as much a hedonistic phenomenon as it is practical and valuable. People won't be as likely to spend money on store-bought bouquets once they learn that they can create flower patches to fill their vases.

When Should Flowers Be Cut?

When a flower is still in the early stages, it is often better to cut it. Make sure to cut them before they are fully opened, and the pollen is visible, even though they should have passed the tight bud stage. The cut garden flowers will keep growing in the vase. The optimum time of day to select flowers is early in the morning or late in the day. If plants are wilting, water them first and then harvest them. Do not cut flowers on a hot summer day.

How Can Cut Flowers Be Made to Last Longer?

- Removing undesirable leaves from stem bases and placing them in a pail of lukewarm water in a cool, shaded area. Some people supplement flowers with food made to nourish them and help stop microorganisms from obstructing their water intake. Keep flowers out of direct sunlight and use clean vases with fresh water.

- Collect vases of all sizes and shapes, and instead of using non-biodegradable florist's foam to hold stems, use traditional "flower frogs" or chicken wire.

Every few days, cut the stems again to extend their life. To stop the spread, constantly prune the flowers to eliminate anything that is drooping or starting to decay. You might utilize a compact set of the best secateurs to do this.

When the water is changed every few days, use flower food, and place the flowers in water that is at an average temperature.

Keep recently cut flowers away from heat sources and direct sunlight. You can add vodka to the water to delay the flower's aging process.

How can tall-stemmed cut garden flowers be prevented from toppling over?

For a cutting garden, we tend to choose taller varieties with longer stems that need support." One approach is to string wide-gapped netting between canes and fasten it over emerging plants at 14 inches (36 cm). Stems pierce the mesh and cover it up. Twigs can support some plants, but tall dahlias and tithonia do best when attached to individual canes.

Avoid overfertilizing plants, as this leads to weak, sappy growth. Too much manure or nitrogen-rich fertilizer will do this. A few high-potash feeds on healthy, well-conditioned soil over the summer will be sufficient.

Printed in Great Britain
by Amazon